CATS IN THE SUN

With love to Spiro and Blossom

PUFFIN PIED PIPER BOOKS
Published by the Penguin Group
Penguin Books USA Inc., 375 Hudson Street, New York, New York, 10014, U.S.A.
Penguin Books Ltd, 27 Wrights Lane, London W8 5TZ, England
Penguin Books Australia Ltd, Ringwood, Victoria, Australia
Penguin Books Canada Ltd, 10 Alcorn Avenue, Toronto, Ontario, Canada M4V 3B2
Penguin Books (N.Z.) Ltd, 182-190 Wairau Road, Auckland 10, New Zealand
Penguin Books Ltd, Registered Offices: Harmondsworth, Middlesex, England

First published in hardcover in the United States 1991 by Dial Books
A Division of Penguin Books USA Inc.

Published in Great Britain by HarperCollins Publishers
Copyright © 1990 by Lesley Anne Ivory
Library of Congress Catalog Card Number: 90-43068
Printed in Hong Kong
First Puffin Pied Piper Printing 1995
ISBN 0-14-055338-X
3 5 7 9 10 8 6 4

A Pied Piper Book is a registered trademark of
Dial Books, a division of Penguin Books USA Inc.,
® TM 1,163,686 and ® TM 1,054,312.

CATS IN THE SUN
is also available in hardcover and miniature editions from
Dial Books.

CATS IN THE SUN

Lesley Anne Ivory

A PUFFIN PIED PIPER

What a happy sight it is to see a cat enjoying the sunshine. Cats adore the sun and seek it everywhere. They appreciate the warmth left by the sun's rays on pebbled paths. They lie in pools of sunlight cast by the winter sun through windows onto rich carpets.

I seek cats wherever I go. Like cats, I also seek warm, sunny places—especially to enjoy holidays in—and I never have difficulty in finding furry friends. I find them on docks watching fishing boats in little Greek harbors . . .

or by the side of small, narrow streets, feeding their kittens in sunny corners.

I love the way the sun shines through their ears, making them seem almost lighted up from within. And I love the way the sun sometimes catches the outline of their fur and whiskers. If you look closely into cats' coats while they are basking in the sunshine, you can see many colors highlighted there, making each hair into a miniature rainbow.

They stretch and wash their faces on doorsteps, walls, and windowsills, enjoying the first rays of the sun, or waiting patiently and hopefully for something interesting to come along. Cats have lots of time.

Butterflies are born into sunlight and fascinate cats who watch them fluttering about, and who then leap like ballet dancers, trying to catch them as they fly. Usually butterflies are just too elusive to be caught, but I have known my little Motley (herself a small tortoiseshell) to successfully bring one down with her paws.

Cats use warm, sunny days as an excuse to sprawl in your best flowers in the garden—preferably catmint which they adore—rolling over and spoiling the shape of the plant by flattening it as they writhe about on their shoulder blades, wild with joy at the fragrant smell of the crushed leaves and flowers.

In North Africa I found two nests of kittens outside one cafe.
One was in a hedge of hibiscus in full bloom, and when
I looked more closely the mother cat looked out and I could
see four little faces peering at me through the exotic flowers.
The other nest was in a tiled recess which had had geraniums,
before the mother cat flattened them to furnish the "cot" for her
babies. I visited this cafe twice a day for a week, for coffee
and tea, but really to see how the kittens were getting on. The
owner of the cafe said, "You can have a kitten, no problem!"
"Oh yes, there is a problem," said my husband.
"She already has twelve at home!"

I have found cats sunbathing on famous, sun-warmed mosaics made by the Romans many years ago. I wonder how many cats have enjoyed the warmth of these little stones, and if they are even aware of the lovely intricate pictures and designs that made the floors of houses in days long past. Ancestral tigers and birds and fish and wonderfully patterned borders are now exposed to the sun, many pieces lost through the ages.

Thousands of miles away in my garden at home, Malteazer is also enjoying the warmth of the sunshine, and rolling over on a mosaic I once made, using little fragments of broken china I found in ploughed fields. My mosaic will not last as long as the Roman ones. It is already cracking, but Malteazer does not mind.

We once shared a lovely picnic on the shore of a Greek island with a
family of cats who kept fetching more and more of their relatives when
they found our picnic sufficiently tasty to be interesting.

Afterward everyone else fell asleep in the shade of a nearby olive tree.
I was looking at the interesting shells and stones and pieces of old pots
half sunken in the warm sand. Some hens and a magnificent cockerel
appeared and joined the cats to help clear up the crumbs, all among the
pink, wild beach flowers and grasses.

At the end of the day when the sun is setting, cats may be seen making
the most of the last little corners still in sunlight, washing their paws
and faces until the shadows lengthen, and the sun slopes around the other
side of the world to awaken all the cats there.

Lesley Anne Ivory

always has her favorite subjects nearby to pose for her: The cats that she uses as models make their home with the popular author and painter. Well-known for her paintings on cards, calendars, and gifts, as well as for her stunningly realistic books, Ms. Ivory's exquisite paintings of cats have gained this unique artist a huge and enthusiastic audience of animal lovers of all ages.

Lesley Anne Ivory lives with her family and twelve cats in Hertfordshire, England.